Ward Schumaker

DANCE!

Harcourt Brace & Company

San Diego New York London

Requests for permission to make copies of any part of the work should be mailed to:
Permissions Department, Harcourt Brace & Company,
6277 Sea Harbor Drive, Orlando, Florida 32887-6777.

Library of Congress Cataloging-in-Publication Data
Schumaker, Ward.
Dance!/Ward Schumaker.—1st ed.
p.   cm.
Summary: A number of animals demonstrate some
of the many different ways to dance, from bumping
and romping to swirls and pliés.
ISBN 0-15-200046-1
[1. Dance—Fiction. 2. Animals—Fiction. 3. Stories in rhyme.]
I. Title.
PZ8.3.S3875Dan   1996
[E]—dc20   95-13697

First edition
A B C D E

Printed in Singapore

The illustrations in this book are six-color hand-separated black ink drawings.
The display and text type were set in Century Old Style by
Harcourt Brace & Company Photocomposition Center, San Diego, California.
Color separations by Bright Arts, Ltd., Singapore
Printed and bound by Tien Wah Press, Singapore
Production supervision by Warren Wallerstein and Pascha Gerlinger
Designed by Ward Schumaker and Lori J. McThomas

Special thanks to Diane D'Andrade and Marcia Wernick

For Matt and my parents
and Hazel in her tutu

I want to jump.

I want to stomp.

I want to bump.

I want to romp.

I want to dance!

Dance like a lady

or a little old man.

Dance in a dragon!

Dance with a fan!

BRAVO!
BRAVO!

... dance in a mask

... dance in the air

. . . dance in a tutu

. . . dance at the fair.

I want to dance!

Dance to a horn!
Dance to a drum.

Dance while I sing,
dance while I hum.

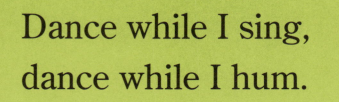

Dance in the darkness.
Dance in the light.

Arms outstretched
or held in tight.

Dance 'neath the sun.
Dance 'neath the moon.

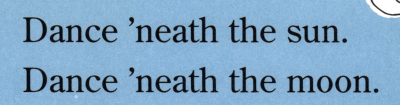

Move like a monkey.
Croon like a loon.

Let's make a circle!

Let's make a square!

Let's make a line that goes nowhere

. . . but—to dance!

Little steps.
Big steps.
Up and down.

Across the porch.
Across the town.

One step forward,
Two steps back.

Clap your hands—
don't lose track.

Plink.

Plank!

Plié.

Plop!

I want to dance until I drop.

Swirl.
Twirl.

Jump and hop.

Up and down.

Flop.

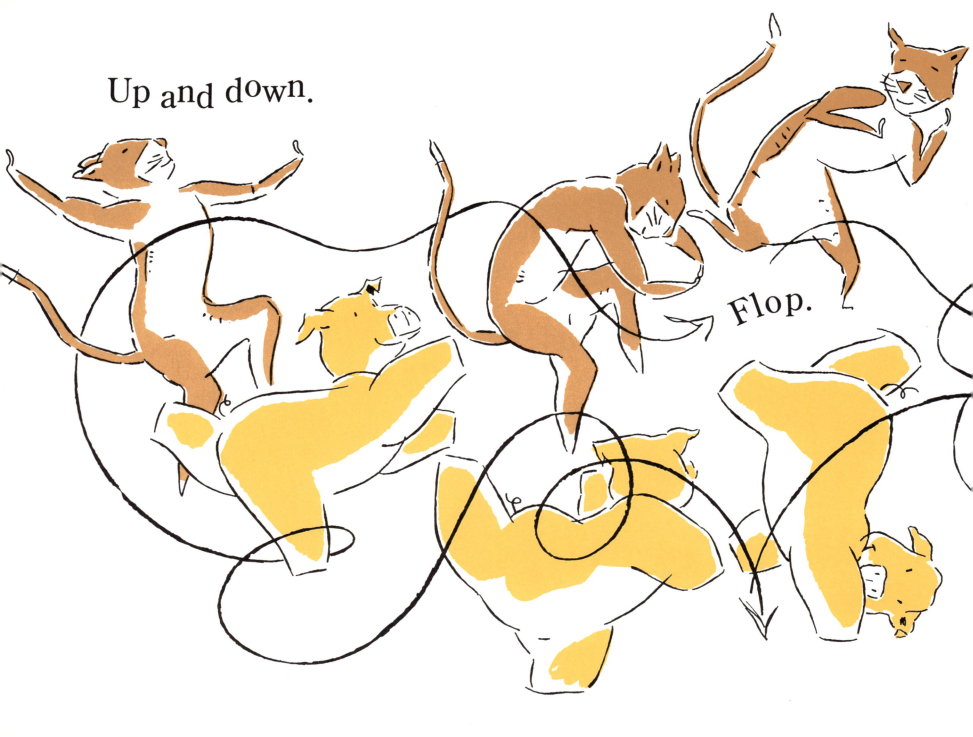

Stop!

Drop.

That's dance.

TONIGHT'S DANCERS:

Timothy Piggot-Smythe

Sylvie LeChat

Irene Pupp

Bruno Pupp

and

The Zoölogical Society Dancers

Even Dancers

Need a Nap.